"Wait a minute!" Sarah-Jane cried. *"That's* not our map! *This* is our map!"

Titus added, "The map you found, Tim—the second map—belongs to someone else."

"I think we'd better take a closer look at this mysterious second map," said Timothy. "Let's take it back to our hideout."

Another case for the T.C.D.C.

THE MYSTERY OF THE

SECOND
MAP

Elspeth Campbell Murphy
Illustrated by Chris Wold Dyrud

Chariot Books
David C. Cook Publishing Co.

A Wise Owl Book
Published by Chariot Books,
an imprint of David C. Cook Publishing Co.
David C. Cook Publishing Co., Elgin, Illinois 60120
David C. Cook Publishing Co., Weston, Ontario

The Mystery of the Second Map
© 1988 by Elspeth Campbell Murphy for text and Chris Wold
Dyrud for illustrations

Cover design by Chris Patchel
First Printing, 1988
Printed in the United States of America
98 97 96 95 94   12 11 10 9 8

Library of Congress Cataloging-in-Publication Data

Murphy, Elspeth Campbell.
    The mystery of the second map.

    (Ten commandments mysteries)
    "A Wise owl book."
    Summary: The suspicions of three cousins about a possible theft
at a building site lead them to prevent a crime and experience the
meaning of the commandment, "You shall have no other gods
before me."
    [1. Ten commandments—Fiction. 2. Cousins—Fiction. 3.
Mystery and detective stories]
I. Dyrud, Chris Wold, ill. II. Title. III. Series: Murphy, Elspeth
Campbell. Ten commandments mysteries.
PZ7.M95316Mygi 1988   [Fic]   87-24919
ISBN 1-55513-526-9

"You shall have no other gods before me."

Exodus 20:3 (NIV)

CONTENTS

AT MISTY PINES CAMPGROUND

Sarah-Jane Cooper was getting a little talking-to. She hadn't done anything wrong. And she wasn't in trouble. But her parents were reminding her of her responsibilities.

The three of them were having breakfast in their cabin at Misty Pines Campground.

Sarah-Jane's cousins, Timothy Dawson and Titus McKay, were staying with them.

But Timothy, who always got up super-early, was already out exploring somewhere.

And Titus, who never got up early if he could help it, was still sound asleep in his bunk bed.

Sarah-Jane's father said, "Your mother and I are going to be really busy building the chapel with the other volunteers, Sarah-Jane. So you and your cousins will be pretty much on your own.

You'll have to entertain yourselves and look out for one another."

Sarah-Jane nodded seriously. "We will."

"Good," said her mother. "Because if we can count on you kids to be responsible, then we can get on with our building work. And if the work goes well, then later on we can take time out for some family fun things."

Sarah-Jane said, "Like—can we go to the Indian Trails souvenir shop in town?"

"Sure," said her father. "We can do that."

"And the Seven Rainbows Waterfall?"

"That, too."

"And can we go for a ride on the Queen-of-the-Lake boat?"

"Yes, indeed."

Sarah-Jane sighed happily. She was sure everything was going to work out great at Misty Pines Campground.

She looked for the hundredth time at the artist's sketch that showed what the chapel her parents were building would be like.

It was going to be a beautiful building. It would have mostly wood and glass walls and even a mostly glass ceiling. So when you sat in the chapel, you would feel like you were part of the woods. It was going to be a wonderful place to worship God.

Sarah-Jane even loved the name of it—The Wayfarer's Chapel.

Her mother had explained to the kids that the word *wayfarer* meant a traveler.

People hiking through the woods could stop at the chapel to rest and think and pray.

Campers could go to worship services there on Sundays.

And people could even use the chapel for weddings. (Sarah-Jane *loved* weddings!)

Sarah-Jane was very proud that her father was in charge of the volunteer builders.

"When are you going to start building?" she asked.

"Some people were delayed in getting here. But I think everybody should arrive by early afternoon," he said. "So I'll get the workers together for a meeting in the lodge after lunch."

Sarah-Jane said, "I wish I could help build the chapel, too!"

"You *will* be helping!" said her mother. "Just knowing that we can count on you kids to be responsible—"

"Helps us more than you know!" finished her father.

Sarah-Jane made a secret promise to herself that she would be *super*-responsible.

She went out on the porch to think about how she and Timothy and Titus could entertain themselves.

She didn't have to wonder long—because she found a mysterious message waiting for her.

2
THE FIRST MAP

The message was written on yellow lined paper. The paper was folded. And it was weighted down by a rock, so it couldn't blow away.

On the outside it said:

TOP SECRET!
PERSONAL!
PRIVATE!

TO T.M. AND S-J.C.,
WHO ARE THE REST OF THE T.C.D.C.!
IF YOU ARE NOT THEM,
YOU ARE NOT ALLOWED
TO OPEN THIS!
SINCERELY,
T.D.

Of course, Sarah-Jane knew that the letters T.C.D.C. stood for the Three Cousins Detective Club. So the paper was a secret message to her and Titus from Timothy.

She quickly unfolded the paper.

Inside there was a note—and a map.

The note said:

Dear S-J and Ti,

I found this neat-O secret hideout. Here's how you get there:

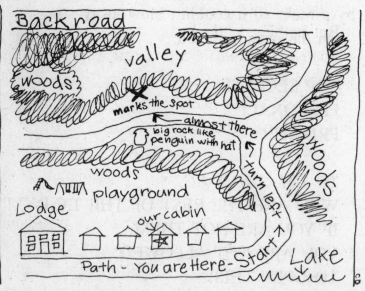

I will wait for you. Hurry up!
Yours truly, Tim.

3
THE SECRET HIDEOUT

Sarah-Jane ran back inside to wake up Titus.

First she called him. Then she shook him. Then she tickled him.

But nothing worked.

So *finally*, Sarah-Jane rinsed out a washcloth in icy cold water and dropped it on Titus's head.

The cold water made Titus wake up crabby. But at least it made him wake up!

And Titus didn't stay crabby for long when he saw Timothy's note. "A secret hideout!" he said. "EXcellent!"

While Titus was getting dressed, Sarah-Jane poured him some milk and juice.

Titus gulped the milk and juice and grabbed a roll to eat on the way.

"OK," said Sarah-Jane, as they tried to hurry

along and study the map at the same time. "Here's the picture of our cabin. We're supposed to follow the footpath until we get to the spot marked with an X."

Titus said, "The X is across from a big rock. Tim says here that the rock looks like a penguin wearing a hat."

"*That* should be easy to find!" said Sarah-Jane. They followed the map quickly but carefully. And at last they came to a big, odd-shaped rock.

"Is that it?" asked Titus. "It looks more like a monkey with a banana on his head."

"No, it doesn't," said Sarah-Jane. "It looks more like a ballerina wearing a crown."

"Well, anyway," said Titus. "It's the only funny-looking rock around here."

"So where's the secret hideout?" asked Sarah-Jane.

"Yeah," said Titus.

"It's so secret even *we* can't find it!"

"Look down!" said a voice. The voice seemed to be coming from behind the low-hanging branches of a huge pine tree.

4
THE WAYFARER'S CHAPEL

Titus and Sarah-Jane stooped down and pushed the branches aside.

And there sat Timothy, looking very pleased with himself. "See?" he said. "The branches make it like a little tent."

He was exactly right. Titus and Sarah-Jane crawled in beside him.

The branches fell back into place. No one could see the detective cousins from the footpath.

"EXcellent hideout, Tim!" exclaimed Titus.

Sarah-Jane took a deep breath of the piney air. "Mmmmm!" she said. "It smells like *Christmas* in here!"

Timothy said, "There's just one little thing you have to watch out for. If you crawl too far over that way, you'll fall off an eNORmous cliff and

kill yourself.''

Right away, Titus and Sarah-Jane crawled over
to see—very carefully.

It turned out Timothy was exaggerating. Their
pine-tree ''tent'' wasn't at the top of a scary cliff.
It was at the top of a gentle little hill.

From this side of the ''tent,'' they could push
aside the branches and look down into a peaceful
little valley.

''Oh, *now* I know where we are!'' cried Sarah-
Jane. ''That little valley is where they're going to
build the Wayfarer's Chapel! See? They even put

up a sign with a picture of how the chapel's going to look. And there are all the piles of building stuff. My dad says the material was delivered over the weekend. Oh, this is *so cool*! We can sit up here in our hideout and watch them work and not even be in the way!''

Sarah-Jane was just explaining to Timothy and Titus about having to be helpful and responsible, when they saw something.

A man was coming down to the building site from the other side of the valley.

5

THE MAN IN THE VALLEY

The man glanced at the chapel sign. Then he walked over to the building materials and looked at them carefully. He even picked up some pieces as if he were getting a feel for them.

"He must be one of the builders," said Sarah-Jane. "He's probably wondering where everyone is. Come on. We can help out by telling him that the get-organized meeting was postponed until this afternoon."

Just for fun, they pretended they were Indian guides and crept silently out of the hideout and down the hill.

The man had his back to them.

"Hi!" said Sarah-Jane.

Obviously the man hadn't heard them coming, because he jumped and whirled around as if someone had set off a firecracker. He dropped the board he was holding and tried to catch his breath.

"Sorry!" exclaimed Timothy. "We didn't mean to scare you!"

"Oh, no, no!" said the man, giving a nervous little laugh. "It's all right. You didn't scare me."

"Anyway," said Sarah-Jane. "I'm Art Cooper's daughter. And we just wanted to tell you that they'll be meeting in the lodge after lunch."

The man looked totally confused. "What? Who?"

"The *builders*," said Sarah-Jane. "Aren't you here to help build the Wayfarer's Chapel?"

"Oh!" said the man. "Oh, I see what you mean. No, I'm not a builder. I'm a—a—preacher!"

Titus said, "Oh, right! Uncle Art told us that the pastors from the nearby towns are going to take turns preaching at the chapel when it's built."

"Yes!" said the man. "Yes! That's it exactly. So I just thought I'd stop by and see how they're getting along."

"They're starting today," said Sarah-Jane. "The lumber and stuff was delivered Saturday."

"Yes, yes. So I see," said the man. "But this isn't a very good place for you to play, is it? I mean, you really shouldn't climb on the piles of lumber. . . ."

"We weren't going to play here," said Titus, sounding surprised that the man would even think that.

Sarah-Jane nodded wisely. "My dad says that building materials cost a fortune these days. We know better than to play with them!"

"We're very responsible," said Timothy.

"Glad to hear it! Glad to hear it!" said the man.

There was an awkward little silence when no one could think of anything else to say.

"Well," said the man at last. "I guess we all have to be going. You have to run along and find a better place to play. And I—uh—have to go work on this week's sermon. Yes—I'm going to preach on the Ten Commandments."

"*All* of them?" asked Sarah-Jane.

"What?" asked the man, sounding confused again.

"That will be a l-o-n-g sermon!" said Titus.

The man laughed and quickly said, "Oh, no, no. Not all ten, no. I'll just start with the first one where it says—um—'God helps those who help themselves.' Well, good-bye. Don't play around here too long!"

And with that, he hurried off through the trees in the direction of the back road.

Timothy, Titus, and Sarah-Jane stood staring after him until he was out of sight.

6
SOMETHING WEIRD

Titus said in a sing-song voice, "Something *weird* is going on around here!"

"Yeah," agreed Timothy. "There's no commandment that says, 'God helps those who help themselves'! Whoever heard of a pastor who doesn't know the Ten Commandments?"

"Yeah," agreed Sarah-Jane. "The First Commandment says, 'You shall have no other gods besides me'! And it means we're supposed to put God first and love Him most of all."

"So why would that guy pretend to be a preacher if he's not one?" asked Titus. "And he sure seemed *nervous*."

"I noticed that, too," said Sarah-Jane thoughtfully. "And he sure didn't seem to want us hanging around here." She sighed. "I was just trying to be helpful and responsible by telling him where the builders' meeting was—and look what happened!''

"It's all right, S-J," said Titus. "It's not *your* fault that something weird is going on around here. You're still a responsible person."

"Ti's right, S-J," said Timothy. "Except I wish you'd be more careful with the hideout map! I mean, what if somebody found it? They'd know right where our hideout is."

"But how could they find the map?" asked Sarah-Jane. "I put it in my pocket."

"Well, it must have dropped out then," said Timothy. "Because—look!"

He stooped down and picked up a piece of yellow lined paper from between two piles of lumber.

Titus and Sarah-Jane crowded around. It was a map all right.

Sarah-Jane shoved her hand deep into her jeans pocket. "Wait a minute!" she cried. "*That's* not our map! *This* is our map!"

Timothy and Titus stared at her in amazement as she pulled out a folded yellow paper.

Quickly she unfolded it. It was Timothy's map, all right.

"But—but—but—" said Timothy.

Titus said, "S-J has *our* map, Tim. The map *you* found—the second map—belongs to somebody else."

"I think we'd better take a closer look at this mysterious second map," said Timothy. "Let's take it back to our hideout."

7
THE SECOND MAP

They split up, and each cousin went back to the hideout by a different way. They didn't really think they were being spied on. But it was more fun being tricky about it.

When they met at the hideout, they studied the paper Timothy had found.

The map showed the main highway. It showed the place where the bumpy road that led through the back of the campground turned off from the main road. It showed the valley. And in the center of the valley there was a great big X.

"That's funny," said Titus. "This map shows where the chapel is going to be."

"What does that note on the bottom say?" asked Sarah-Jane.

It took them awhile to figure it out, because the

note was written in scribbly cursive.

It said:

Joe—

Here's how to get to the site I was telling you about. You won't believe how good the stuff is. We'd better move fast. I'll meet you with the truck at eight o'clock Monday morning.

Dan.

The cousins looked at one another in bewilderment.

Timothy said, "What's going on? Whose map is this?"

Titus said, "It looks like a grown-up drew this map. A grown-up named Dan drew this map for another grown-up named Joe. Probably Joe used this map to find the valley. So he's the one who dropped it there—where you found it, by the lumber piles."

"OK, that makes sense," said Timothy. "But who's Joe? Is he one of the builders?"

Sarah-Jane shook her head. "I doubt it. My dad sent maps to all the volunteers. But he

Xeroxed them. This map is written in pen by somebody named Dan—not Art. Besides, why would one of my dad's builders get here so early?''

''What time is it?'' asked Titus.

Sarah-Jane looked at her watch. (Usually she didn't wear a watch when she was playing outside at home. But she had more responsibility at Misty Pines.) ''It's a quarter to eight,'' she said.

''OK,'' said Titus slowly. ''So something is going to happen in fifteen minutes—at eight o'clock. But *what*?''

Timothy said, "And we still don't know who Joe is. . . . Hey! Wait a minute! I bet he's that guy we just met down there! I bet he dropped the map when we scared him."

"I think you're onto something, Tim!" cried Titus. "That guy said he wasn't a builder. And we're pretty sure he lied about being a pastor. So the question is—what was he doing with a map showing how to get to the chapel?"

"Do you think he and Dan are spies?" asked Sarah-Jane. "Or maybe burglars?"

"Maybe they're going to steal something really big," said Timothy. "Maybe that's why they need a truck."

"But what's there to steal around here?" asked Titus, with a shrug.

"Oh, *no*!" cried Sarah-Jane.

"What? WHAT!" said her cousins.

"The lumber and stuff! *That's* what they're going to steal! My dad says it's a terrible problem whenever he's building houses. People sneak up to the development and take the materials for themselves."

"Yes, but this lumber is for a *church*!" said Timothy. "How could people steal from a *church*?"

Titus said, "It—it would be like they were robbing . . . *God*!"

"I know!" said Sarah-Jane desperately. "But some people don't *care* what God thinks! My Sunday school teacher says if you care about something more than God, it's like you're worshiping a phony little god instead of the *real* One! It's like you're putting yourself first instead of putting God first. I don't think Dan and Joe care about God *or* the chapel! I think they're just going to take the building stuff for themselves!"

Titus gulped and said to Timothy, "S-J is right, Tim! I think she's figured out exactly what's going to happen. We've got to *do* something!

And we've got to do it FAST!''

They decided that Timothy was the one to go get help. He was the fastest runner of the three, and he had already found some shortcuts through the woods.

So he stuffed Dan's map into his pocket and raced off to show Uncle Art.

9
THE LOOKOUTS

Meanwhile, Titus and Sarah-Jane crawled over to the valley side of the hideout.

Breathlessly they kept a lookout over the building materials that would one day become the Wayfarer's Chapel.

Suddenly Titus whispered, "Look! There's Joe! He's back, and he's looking around."

"He's looking for us," whispered Sarah-Jane. "He wants to make sure we went away like he told us to."

"He can't see us up here," said Titus softly. "What time is it?"

Sarah-Jane glanced at her watch. "Eight o'clock!" she replied. And she thought to herself, "Oh, hurry, Tim! *Hurry*!"

Just then they saw Joe turn and walk up the hill

toward the back road.

"S-J! Do you hear that? It's the truck!"

"Yes, I hear it, too. And I can *see* it now!" said Sarah-Jane. "They're backing it up as close as they can to the valley. Oh, Ti! What are we going to do? What if they load up the truck and drive away before Tim gets back with my dad?"

Titus bit his lip as they watched Dan and Joe begin to carry the building supplies away from the chapel site.

"OK, here's the plan," Titus said. "It will take awhile for them to load up the truck. But Tim might not get back in time. So we have to sneak around to the back road and write down the license plate number of the truck."

"We can't let them see us!" squeaked Sarah-Jane.

"No, we can't," said Titus. "So we have to be super-careful."

"OK," said Sarah-Jane, taking a deep breath. "Do you have something to write with?"

Titus dug deep into his pockets. He came up with some string, a marble, a stick of gum, a quarter, and finally the little stub of a pencil.

"Good!" said Sarah-Jane. "And we can use Tim's map for the paper."

Silently, they pushed the branches aside and crept out onto the footpath.

Sarah-Jane's feelings were all mixed up inside her. She was glad Titus had thought of this plan. But the plan made her nervous.

Going as quickly and as quietly as they could— not talking at all—they followed the footpath as it curved around the valley and joined up with the back road.

Suddenly, just ahead of them, they saw the red

truck.

They each motioned to the other one to duck behind the bushes.

Titus peeked out just enough to copy down the license plate number—and to note the make of the truck.

Then Sarah-Jane peeked out just enough to double-check what Titus had written. Everything checked out. Now all they could do was wait.

Even though she and Titus were well hidden by the bushes, Sarah-Jane couldn't help wishing that she and her cousins were back in the hideout. Again she thought to herself, "Oh, hurry, Tim! *Hurry*!"

At that moment, they heard the sound of many running feet. And suddenly it seemed as if the whole valley were full of people.

Dan was surrounded. Caught red-handed.

But Joe, who was closer to the truck, jumped in and roared away.

Sarah-Jane and Titus burst out of the bushes and charged down the hill.

"Daddy!" cried Sarah-Jane. "Here we are!"

"Tim!" yelled Titus. "You made it!"

The three cousins rushed together, all gasping for breath and all talking at once.

Timothy said, "First I told Uncle Art. And then he told some other people. But I guess we didn't get here fast enough, because Joe got away!"

"Joe won't get far!" said Sarah-Jane. "We got the license plate number!"

"Yes," said Titus. "And we can describe him

and the truck."

"Neat-O!" cried Timothy. "Aunt Sue stayed behind to call the police. They'll be here any minute. Good work, Ti and S-J!"

"Good work, Tim!" said Titus and Sarah-Jane.

Then Titus added, "It just goes to show—you can depend on the T.C.D.C.!"

"What's a 'teesy-deesy'?" asked one of the builders.

"It's letters," explained Sarah-Jane. "Capital T.

Capital C.

Capital D.

Capital C.

It stands for the Three Cousins Detective Club.''

"Hey, everybody!" Uncle Art called to the workers. "Have you met these kids? My very responsible nephews, Timothy Dawson and Titus McKay. And here is my very responsible daughter, Sarah-Jane Cooper!"

Everybody burst into applause. (Everybody, that is, except Dan.)

Timothy and Titus smiled at the applause and took big, sweeping bows.

But Sarah-Jane said, "Oh, *Daddy*! I'm so embarrassed, I could just *DIE*!"

"Don't be silly, Sarah-Jane," said her father. "You deserve to take a bow!"

Sarah-Jane couldn't help smiling. "Oh, well," she said. "If you insist. . . ."

The End

THE TEN COMMANDMENTS MYSTERIES

When Timothy, Titus, and Sarah-Jane, the three cousins, get together the most ordinary events turn into mysteries. So they've formed the T.C.D.C. (That's the Three Cousins Detective Club.)

And while the three cousins are solving mysteries, they're also learning about the Ten Commandments and living God's way.

You'll want to solve all ten mysteries along with Sarah-Jane, Ti, and Tim:

The Mystery of the Laughing Cat—"You shall not steal." *Someone stole rare coins. Can the cousins find the thief?*

The Mystery of the Messed-up Wedding—"You shall not commit adultery." *Can the cousins find the missing wedding ring?*

The Mystery of the Gravestone Riddle—"You shall not murder." *Can the cousins solve a 100-year-old murder case?*

The Mystery of the Carousel Horse—"You shall not covet." *Why does the stranger want an old, wooden horse?*

The Mystery of the Vanishing Present—"Remember the Sabbath day and keep it holy." *Can the cousins figure out who has Grandpa's missing birthday gift?*

The Mystery of the Silver Dolphin—"You shall not give false testimony." *Who's telling the truth—and who's lying?*

The Mystery of the Tattletale Parrot—"You shall not misuse the name of the Lord your God." *What will the beautiful green parrot say next?*

The Mystery of the Second Map—"You shall have no other gods before me." *Can the cousins discover who dropped the strange map?*

The Mystery of the Double Trouble—"Honor your father and your mother." *How could Timothy be in two places at once?*

The Mystery of the Silent Idol—"You shall not make for yourself an idol." *If the idol could speak, what would it tell the cousins?*

Available at your local Christian bookstore.

David C. Cook Publishing Co., Elgin, IL 60120

SHOELACES AND BRUSSELS SPROUTS

One little lie, but BIG trouble!

When Alex lies to her mom about losing her shoelaces, it doesn't seem like a big deal. But how do you replace special baseball laces when you don't have any money and you're not allowed to go to the store alone? A big softball game is coming up, and Alex knows the coach won't let her pitch in shoes without laces—or in cowboy boots!

Every kid gets into the predicaments that Alex does—ones that start out small and mushroom. Readers will learn from Alex's mistakes and understand that they have the same sources of help that she turns to: A God who loves them and wants to help them, and parents who understand.

Other books in the Alex Series . . .

2 *French Fry Forgiveness*—Sometimes making friends is harder than making enemies.

3 *Hot Chocolate Friendship*—Is winning first place as important to Alex as being a friend?

4 *Peanut Butter and Jelly Secrets*—Obeying her parents (even in little things) beats the awful results of disobeying.

Available at your local Christian bookstore.

David C. Cook Publishing Co.
850 N. Grove Ave.
Elgin, IL 60120

Chariot Books

If you liked this book, you'll also want to solve all the Beatitudes Mysteries along with Sarah-Jane, Titus, and Timothy:

The Mystery of the Empty School
"Blessed are the meek"
The Mystery of the Candy Box
"Blessed are the merciful"
The Mystery of the Disappearing Papers
"Blessed are the pure in heart"
The Mystery of the Secret Snowman
"Blessed are the peacemakers"
The Mystery of the Golden Pelican
"Blessed are those who mourn"
The Mystery of the Princess Doll
"Blessed are those who are persecuted"
The Mystery of the Hidden Egg
"Blessed are the poor in spirit"
The Mystery of the Clumsy Juggler
"Blessed are those who hunger and thirst for righteousness"